A Peculiar People

By Dr. Larry G. Morgan

Published by Morgan Publishing, LLC, 6665 N NC Hwy 109, Winston-Salem, NC 27107   336-769-2210

All rights reserved. No part of this book may be reproduced in any form or by any electronic or mechanical means including information storage and retrieval systems without permission in writing from its publisher, Morgan Publishing LLC, or its author.

ISBN No.: 978-1974065868

Dedication

This book is dedicated to my sister, Joan Morgan Rudisill, who first aroused my interest in the Melungeons.

Preface

I don't remember exactly when I first learned of the Melungeons. Several years ago my sister, Joan Morgan Rudisill, went on a mission trip to the area of upper east Tennessee for a few weeks. There in the middle of Melungeon country, she learned of the Melungeons. When she returned to her home, she called me on the phone and asked me what I knew of this strange group of people. As a result of our conversation, she sent me a packet of information that she had discovered while in Tennessee concerning the Melungeons. I studied the information, then laid it aside and eventually lost it. However, my interest in the Melungeons had been aroused, and from time to time I thought of them. For several years, I considered writing a book based on the legend of the Melungeons. Here is the book. I truly hope you enjoy it.

Dr. Larry G. Morgan

Prologue

Although the actual writing of this book was rather easy and a pleasure, I found myself in a dilemma. The narrative in this book takes place before there were any geographical names to the surface features such as mountains and rivers. (All of the places I describe in the book are actual geographical sites). Was I to break the progress and flow of the story from the perspective of the characters by identifying the geographical features as they became part of the story? I decided not to do this. Rather, I decided to try to subtly identify the surface features by clues in the narrative without identifying them with their modern names. One example of this is my description of what obviously was Pilot Mountain. Another example is the Uwharrie Mountains. The reader should also know that the last names of the characters in my story are the names of

Melungeon families that are still native to the area described in the story.

(Note to reader: For literary purposes, at times I refer to the entire group of characters as "whites" even though two of them are black).

Table of Contents

Chapter	Title	Page
1	On the Beach	9
2	The Decision	20
3	The Departure	28
4	The Hurricane	33
5	What about Food?	36
6	The Hunt	39
7	Indians	47
8	The Great River	56
9	The Devil	59
10	Death of a Compatriot	61
11	The First Mountain	65
12	Old Lucifer	66
13	The First River	68
14	Another River and Another Mountain	73
15	In Custody	77
16	The Showdown	82
17	To Go or to Stay	85

Introduction

In the Bible in Titus 2: 14, Christians are referred to as "a peculiar people." In the area of the Cumberland Gap near the juxtaposition of the four states of North Carolina, Tennessee, Kentucky, and Virginia dwells another "peculiar people." Today, they are generally found in Hancock and Hawkins counties of northeastern Tennessee and nearby areas in southeast Kentucky and Lee County in southwest Virginia. These are collectively called the Melungeons. They are a conglomeration of white, black, and Native American descent. They are mostly light-skinned to darker shades of color, and do not fit into any known ethnic group. They obviously are of mixed racial ancestry. Because of certain words in their language, they are most likely of southern Europe and northern Africa origin, Portuguese being one of the most prominent representatives. They were often referred to as "Turks, "Moors," or "Portuguese" by the surprised, early, settlers who found a thriving community of these "peculiar people" in the 17th Century. Many of the Melungeons claim to be both Indian and Portuguese. One example was "Spanish Peggy" Gibson, wife of Vardy Gibson. Whatever their origin, there seems to be general agreement among researchers that there was definitely a pronounced mixing of Iberian (Spanish and/or Portuguese) and African influences in the genetic makeup of the Melungeons. One historian has noted that some early slaves and free blacks were "Atlantic Creoles," mixed-race descendants of Iberian and African women or slaves. Many were bilingual, speaking both English and Portuguese. The Melungeons maintained their mixed, racial ancestry until around 1900 by marrying within their ethnic group.

World War I brought the problem of their ancestry to a jolt because the draftees did not know how to list their race on the military forms. Another "modern" problem that had to be confronted was how to classify them as to race for purposes of taxation, whether black, white, Indian, or even mulatto. In several court cases down through the years the Melungeons were repeatedly certified as to the legitimacy of their white race. Some prominent Melungeon family names today are Collins, Gibson and Mullins. There are several notable public figures that are of Melungeon ancestry. One of these notables is Colonel Francis Gary Powers from the little town of Pound, in southwest Virginia, the U-2 pilot who was shot down over the Soviet Union during President Eisenhower's second administration.

Some Melungeon families have also been traced to Ashe County in northwestern North Carolina.

Generally, for most of their history in the United States, with the exception of the period from 1834 to 1865, which was associated with the Nat Turner slave rebellion, they have enjoyed basically the same rights as whites. For example, they held property, voted, and served in the army. Some even owned slaves before the Civil War. However, at times they were discriminated against as "people of color," and were not allowed to attend public schools.

As for their everyday life, the Melungeons have maintained a life style much as the whites since their beginning. They have lived in modest log cabins and planted permanent crops in that small part of the country. Pictures exist of some of these ancient dwellings to this day. One example is Malala Mullin's cabin located in Vardy, Blackwater

Creek in Tennessee. It is reported that in the late 1800s and 1900s, the predominant religious denomination was Baptist.   There are three main theories concerning the origin of this people. The first one, and latest, is that the Melungeons were the result of early settlers and explorers who simply migrated there from very early colonial settlements, particularly in Virginia. These included free blacks and white people who intermarried with the local Native Americans and with each other. There, they formed a close-knit family and closed economic system with little or no contact with the outside world.

Given the dearth of the recorded presence of Portuguese and Spanish settlers among the early English and other European immigrants to the American English colonies, this theory loses some of it legitimacy. That reasonably significant numbers of these two groups would wind up in the same general location without any pre-planning and co-ordination beggars the imagination.

Another theory concerning the origin of these strange people, the Melungeons, is that they were almost entirely of Spanish origin. The Spanish established bases, or settlements, all along the southeastern coast of the United States from North Carolina to Florida. Some of these outposts were several miles inland. As pressure from the English colonies to the north in the 1600s mounted, with the expectation that they would be unable to protect them, the Spanish began to withdraw these isolated outposts. One theory is that due to the difficulty of communication and other problems some of the more isolated outposts in the Carolinas, especially North Carolina, simply "didn't get the word," and, as a result, were left to their own devices. Somehow or other, these abandoned "settlers," comprised of mostly Spanish and Spanish and a few blacks, made contact with the Indians of the region under discussion and intermarried and prospered.

I don't believe this theory is very likely considering the wilderness of the region in the 1500s and 1600s. Also, if the Spanish had been the only source of the white skin people, the people would have been speaking pure Spanish. This is not the case. Little or no Spanish was being spoken by these people when they were discovered. However, Portuguese was very often a second language to the English spoken by these people when they were discovered.

Even a theory that the ancient Phoenicians were responsible for this group of people due to their proclivity for exploration of the world has been promulgated by a few free thinkers. Even the so-called lost continent of Atlantis has been offered as the origin of the Melungeons. I have no comment but to say anything is possible, I suppose.

There is one other plausible theory, which is the basis for this book.

Chapter 1

On the Beach

The time was 1576. There were ten of them in the little camp back under the live oak trees on the North Carolina beach: one from Portugal, one from Spain, and two black Moors from North Africa who spoke Portuguese. One was a Frenchman, and the rest were from the docks of London, England. They ranged in age from sixteen years to thirty-two years. For the previous two weeks or so, things had been going fairly well. They had sufficient shelter from the late afternoon thunder storms, because the center of the camp was the rather spacious, make-shift, tent. It was concocted from a piece of topsail tied at each corner to a sturdy limb of four different, low-hanging, live oak trees, because there was not available a longer tent, ridge pole from the stunted, crooked, live oak trees.

At least the captain of their ship had been kind and thoughtful enough to row them around the southern tip of the outer banks islands and across the inlet to the mainland proper before they had had to disembark the large rowboat. Also, the captain had allowed them to take with them as much of their personal belongings that could fit into the boat along with the nine other passengers. The ten had also taken as much biscuit, hardtack, salt pork, and jerky as they could carry. Other than the two small axes and a Dutch oven and large skillet, perhaps the most important items were the two muskets and a good supply of powder and shot the captain had supplied. With what food they had carried with them, they were set to survive for a month or two at the least. There were several flint boxes scattered throughout the ten which had already come into good use for cooking the marine species they managed to hook. Also of great use and importance were the knives in the belts that almost all of them carried for various uses, not the least of which was cleaning the fish they caught and the animals they killed.

Another valuable commodity that several of the ten had were several fish hooks and strings. With these tied to make-shift fishing poles, they supplied themselves with fresh fish almost daily. These fish, along with the crab and clams they harvested routinely, kept them in relatively good health and good spirits.

"How long have we been at this location?" Tom Collins, the sixteen year old former cabin boy of no one in particular asked, standing and squinting into the early afternoon, July sun.

"About two weeks, or more, but specifically, fifteen and a half days," replied Luke Gibson, sitting flat on the beach with his ankles crossed letting sand sift slowly through his hands.

"Well, that means we've only got about fifteen more days in this God-forsaken land," growled Isaiah Mullins, biggest man of the ten, being a shade over six feet, five inches tall and weighing a solid 210 pounds. He grimaced as he tried to shave a knot off of the short stick he aimlessly whittled on. Then, he spat to the side, threw the stick to the sand, and sat down. The two black Moors, who spoke Portuguese were wrestling with a sand shark about four or five feet long in the shallow surf immediately in front of the tent and the unoccupied, former, fellow shipmates. Three more sat several feet away beneath yet another live oak tree and talked quietly among themselves.

Until fifteen days ago, the ten beach combers had been aboard an English battleship-of-the-line that was searching out rich Spanish and Portuguese treasure galleons bound for the ports of Spain and Portugal loaded with the gold and silver they had stolen from the hapless natives of Central and South America which they claimed possession of. Most had been roustabouts hired on to perform the support roles of cooks, cleaners, and caretakers of the huge eight and ten pounder cannons, powder, and balls. Three had been pressed-ganged into the King's navy.

For almost a week they had been in sight of three of these treasure ships, but there was one, grave, problem. They were escorted by three other huge, top-of-the-line Spanish war ships, stripped and ready for battle. The captain had called them all together and advised them peremptorily that they would just be in the way when the attack began, and throughout the impending battle. He proposed to set them ashore for the time being and return for them in thirty days after gloriously winning the battle and loaded with the gold and silver coins and bars. Henceforth, they had gathered their personal items and collected the axes and muskets loaded with all the food stuffs they could carry, embarked rather haphazardly into the large life boat, and had been rowed to the mainland shore.

It was mid-July, and the first fifteen days ashore had been very predictable; rather warm at night and in the early mornings, and hot as hades the rest of the day. Over all, the weather had not been a problem. Except for a few late afternoon showers, the weather had been perfect with the temperature rising into the low to mid-nineties in the afternoons. The large piece of sail had adequately protected them from the heat of the day and from the afternoon thunder showers. They had not yet felt the hunger pains they would experience later on due to the hardtack, jerky, salt pork, and biscuit from the ship's larder supplemented by the marine life they managed to harvest. Squadrons of pelicans had periodically sailed smoothly, serenely and silently up and down the beach. Gulls had argued and fought over the bits of uneaten food the men had tossed in the air, and porpoises had arched against the horizon just beyond the breakers almost every day. Except for the slowly rising anxiety in almost every one of them, as the days and nights slowly passed, all was serene. All of them were confident that the sails of the ship that had set them ashore would top the horizon any day now, and they would soon be safe aboard again. Little did they know that the sea battle had not gone well, and that that certain vessel would never come back for them because the hull was now lying on the bottom of the Atlantic Ocean with two huge, cannon-blasted holes just below its water line.

By the twenty-fifth day of their stay on the beach, tensions were rising steadily and tempers were beginning to be short. The men spent an exorbitant amount of time just staring out at the ocean's horizon singly and in groups of three or four talking in subdued tones.

By the thirtieth day, the men were getting up early and checking their gear for a quick trip. That they were nervous and anxious was evident, but they were not yet panic-stricken. They realized that the dates for departure and arrival of ships was almost never on time. Most were ready to accept a few more days for the ship that would take them back to civilization.

By the tenth day of the overdue vessel, the supplies of hardtack, salt pork, jerky, and ship's biscuit were practically non-existent. The men were restricted to eating the fish caught by the men with the fish hooks and lines, and the shell creatures caught by hand. They had also taken to maintaining a smoky fire made of the scarce driftwood and dead branches from the dense undergrowth on the beach during the daylight hours hoping that any vessel passing by would see it and rescue them. To create great clouds of smoke, they added the green, leafy, ends of small branches cut from the live oak trees nearby to the flames.

At the end of twenty days of the overdue rescue ship, the anxiety and nervousness of the now castaways was rapidly nearing despair.

At the dawning of the twenty-first overdue day, before the rest of the men had awakened, Luke Gibson reached over and shook his neighbor out of his repose. "Caleb. Caleb. Wake up and come with me to get a drink of water." Luke spoke very quietly so as not to wake anyone else.

Caleb grunted awake and struggled to his feet. "What's that you're saying, Luke?"

"Let's walk over to the stream where we can talk privately," replied Luke softly.

Once at the stream and each having had a drink from their cupped hands, Luke began. "It's evident that we are going to have to do something drastic, or we will all soon perish here on this God-forsaken beach. It's obvious that the ship is not going to return for us. It may have gone down in a violent storm, or worse, been sunk by the Spanish navy. Anyway, it's not coming."

Caleb replied softly, "Well, what are we to do?"

"We need to get the others together to discuss this situation that we are all in equally," replied Luke.

"Well, let's get to it," Caleb replied, turning to walk over to where most of the other men were sleeping.

Chapter 2

The Decision

As they approached the sleeping men, Luke spoke with a loud voice. "Okay. It's time to rise and shine, you landlubbers." He nudged one sleeping form hesitant to rise with the toe of his boot. "Come on, get up," he repeated authoritatively.

Once all the men were up and assembled, Luke began. "It's become common sense to all of us that we are not going to be picked up by a ship. We've got to do something. So what are your ideas and suggestions?"

One of the black Moors, Abbad, spoke up in a broken mixture of Portuguese and

English. "Seeing that we are all sea men, I propose we try to escape by sea."

"And just how are we supposed to do that? that? Swim?" Rafael El Largo, the Portuguese, replied sarcastically.

"We build a giant raft from the pine trees that begin a couple of hundred yards inland from where we are now standing," returned Abbad also speaking in a smattering of Portuguese and English.

"And how are we going to hold the trunks together, seeing that we have no rope?" questioned Raphael.

"We'll have to locate some sturdy vines to do it with. But it can be done. Furthermore, we can fashion a tent of the old sail to shield us from the worst weather," replied Abbad.

"And how do you propose to steer the monstrosity," asked Tom Collins, the youngest.

"We can make oars from the smaller trees that will do the job adequately. All we will need them for is to row us out into the area we are most likely to see a ship. Once there, we lay-to and wait. We can survive on the fish we will catch," replied Abbad.

"That idea has possibilities, but it has its faults also. For example, suppose no ship ever comes by, and that is not unlikely due to the fact that that part of the ocean is not in the major sea lanes of the Atlantic, as of the present. And certainly we would be at the mercy of the elements all of the time. Furthermore, where would we get enough drinking water to survive? Only so much rain water can be recovered at a time," said Luke Gibson.

The Spaniard, Pedro Gonzalez, spoke next. "In Seville, I have heard of a large river to the west. One of my countrymen, Hernando De Soto, led an expedition in the 1540s from Florida north for several hundred miles many years ago, and then turned west. He is the source of the information about the great river. He did not say how long it took him to reach the river, though."

Le Bon, the Frenchman spoke up. "I, to, have heard of a great river to the west. I propose we head west into the forest and the land mass. From the maps I have seen to date, somewhere to the west a great river does flows south. Somewhere along it, and especially at its mouth, there are bound to be outposts of the Spanish. Falling into the hands of the Spanish can't be any worse that dying from drinking salt water and burning to death in the hot sun."

"How far west is this great river?" came a voice in the group.

"Who can say for sure?" someone answered.

Le Bon continued, "In the forest we can find shelter from the storms and food and fresh water enough. With the muskets we can bring down deer and bears, and small game, and we will be able to find food from the land such as apples, plums, berries and so on."

"There is a third option also," spoke up Caleb Goins.

"And what might that be," asked someone in the group.

"We can go south and follow the coast line to the Spanish settlements in Florida. The only problem is we know that is a far piece," offered Caleb Goins. "If we stay relatively close to the coastline, we will always have a source of food, that is, fish and other aquatic life. Fresh water is also assured."

"Considering the fact that we know how long and treacherous the way to Florida is, and the great river may be just over the horizon, it seems that the way west is the best answer," replied Luke Gibson. "Does anyone else have a suggestion of a better route than has already been discussed? The northern route is out of consideration as there are not any settlements we know of along the northern coast. Okay. Let's put it to a vote."

Two voted to go to sea on the raft, two voted to take the south trip to Florida, and the other six voted to try the way west. The matter was settled. They would go west.

"Well, that settles it. We'll go west. The vote doesn't mean you have to go. If you want to go south to Florida, go. If you want to go by way of the ocean, go. If you choose to go with the six of us, all we ask is that you do your part of the work and other duties that may arise as we go along," replied Luke Gibson who was now the apparent leader of the group. "It's early today. If it is okay with you, let's take this day to get ready, that is, pack up our gear, catch what fish we can and clams and lobsters. Then, we can get started early in the morning. Let's all leave in the morning as surfeited with food as we can hold because it may be a goodly time before we have an opportunity to fill up again. Try to go to sleep early so you will be as rested as possible. We will alternate carrying the two cooking utensils, the piece of sail, the two axes, and the muskets. We'll use the piece of sail for a tent for shelter, if we ever have to. Crossing the streams and small rivers shouldn't be too difficult because this hot weather has cut their volume greatly.

That night the men retired early, but most found it difficult to fall asleep. Finally, though, all was still and quiet, and the talking gradually ceased.

Chapter 3

The Departure

The next morning dawned much the same as most of the others; the huge orange orb of the sun was just rising over the eastern horizon, the tide was coming in, and the waves crashed onto the shore with unusual power and noise. Everyone seemed eager to get started.

As the last person loaded up with his Spartan belongings and gathered spontaneously into a coherent unit, Luke Gibson, his voice rising loud enough to silence the other nine, spoke. "Men and friends, I think it only fit for us to pause and call on the Almighty. As none of us are of a religious nature, I will pray, if that is okay with you? Let's all remove our hats and bow our heads. Our Heavenly Father, today we are about to embark on an uncertain and unknown journey. We ask that you guide us, help us to make the right decisions, and keep us safe. May we eventually locate the great river that will bring us to safety at last. Amen."

"Before we leave, I suggest we leave some kind of a signal to people who may finally get here as to what happened to us. I propose we carve 'gone west' into a tree so that others may know what happened to us," interjected one of the Englishmen, John Powell

"That's a good idea. Will you do it, John?" replied Luke Gibson.

"Sure, as soon as we get to a tree large enough to accommodate both of the words," John replied.

"Well, let's go," someone intoned in a positive tone.

Luke Gibson started down the beach to locate a reasonable opening in the dense undergrowth that would lead them west into the longleaf pine forest, and the others, one by one, fell into a single file behind him. After about two hundred yards, there loomed a large, isolated sycamore which they would pass close by. The group paused long enough for John to carve the words 'gone west' into its thin, tough, greenish-white, bark. No one ever saw it again because the next hurricane would snap the trunk off just where the words were carved, and they would fall into the mud where the great bole would decay.

The men were in good humor this morning as they walked single file through the low shrubs and live oak trees. They were careful to hold the limbs so that they did not sweep back and give the person behind a sharp swat. Most of them were optimistic and in reasonably good spirits brought on simply by the knowledge they were finally taking their fate into their own hands. No more sitting on the beach waiting for a ship that would never come.

Soon, the low shrubs and live oak trees began to give way to the land of longleaf pines. Here, undergrowth practically disappeared, so more rapid progress was possible. The birds, however, were much disturbed with loud squawking and shrill whistling. Occasionally squirrels scolded them from high branches as they extracted the pine seeds from the cones, and rabbits scurried out of their path. All of the men were able to keep up because their ages ranged from the sixteen year old cabin boy, Tom Collins, to Luke Gibson, who was thirty-two years of age and the former boat-wright for Sir Francis Drake's ship, the Golden Hind. Most of them were in relatively good physical condition, although many of them had lost a few pounds due to the scarcity of good food while on the beach, especially during the days after the expected arrival of the rescue ship.

It was on the fifth day of their trek into the hinterland when the gray clouds began to build up from the southeast. By night fall a strong wind had blown up and was constantly increasing in volume. The rain began. Soon, the rain came down as if someone was empting a huge pail.

Chapter 4

The Hurricane

"Quickly, now!" shouted Luke Gibson. "Get the sail set up as a tent with two sides. You men with the axes cut down that small pine over there for a ridgepole, and several smaller, shorter, pieces to stake the edges to the ground!"

As the men worked feverishly to unwind the piece of material that they had not used on the trip as yet, others began to hack at a small pine and trim the limbs off for a makeshift, tent ridge pole. After lodging both ends in adjacent low limbs from two mature trees, they hurriedly threw the sail across it and secured the sides with the short stakes driven into the edge of the sail and into the ground. Now, the worst of the gale and rain was prevented from striking them directly. But another danger became evident. Limbs and entire trees began to be snapped and even uprooted by the fierce storm. What would they do if the very trees to which their makeshift tent was attached should be toppled over? The party found themselves in the path of a hurricane from the Caribbean Sea that had formed off of the west coast of Africa, gradually moved west across the warm, tropical, ocean, but had been turned north by the Leeward Islands. It had skirted the southeast coast and had finally made landfall somewhere just to the south of the beach where they had been marooned. After several hours, the wind suddenly died down and the rain stopped. Even the sun was shining relatively brightly. The men all exited the tent thankful that the violent storm had passed. However, much to the surprise of the castaways, the wind and rain began again in earnest, but from the opposite direction. (Fortunately, the dense grove of trees the tent was pitched in blocked off much of the force of the wind and the rain.) Once more, the men dove for the safety of their makeshift tent. If anything, this storm was more intense than it had been before. The men huddled as closely as possible and uttered silent prayers for their safety. The sound of breaking timber was now louder and more frequent than before. At times, it seemed the entire tent with its occupants would be blown to the four winds. But, to their great relief, after a few hours of this calamity, the wind began to die down, the driving rain ceased its violent downpour to lighter and lighter showers, and soon had ceased completely. Little did they know that they had survived one of the most violent displays of nature; a category one tropical hurricane.

Chapter 5

What about Food?

By now another dire situation had arisen. Food. Hunger. The slight provisions they had brought with them from the beach had all but vanished, and starvation stared them in the face.

"We should have just stayed on the beach. At least, we would not have starved!" announced Abraham Goodman, one of the three pressed-ganged sailors from the bars and docks of London, so loudly everyone was sure to hear, especially Luke Gibson, the de facto leader.

Soon, others were chiming in also. "Yeah. He's right. We'd all be better off back there."

"Well," replied Luke. If that's what you want, you're welcome just to sashay your behinds back to the hot sand and another great storm."

"Just what are we going to do?" Inquired Pedro Gonzalez, the Spaniard in the entourage in broken Spanish and English, and with a desperate lilt in his voice.

"Well, just about all we can do is send out our two best marksman with the two muskets and a couple or three rounds and powder and hope and pray they can bring down a deer or a wild turkey. That might be enough to keep us from starving for the present, anyway," replied Luke without much conviction in his voice.

"Yeah. That's a good suggestion. We've seen a lot of sign along the way. Early morning or the last hour of daylight is best, but you may see a deer at any time of day," answered the Spaniard, Pedro Gonzalez.

"But the drawback is that we others will have to stay in camp until the hunters are successful, so we'll lose all of that traveling time," someone proffered.

"Well, it has to be done, so let's just plan on it for tomorrow," said Luke Gibson with a note of finality in his voice.

Chapter 6

The Hunt

The following morning dawned misty and damp. It would be a couple of hours before the sun could dissipate the morning mist. Caleb Goins and Isiah Mullins, the appointed hunters, rose before any of the others, loaded their muskets, and then disappeared into the fog as silently as ghosts. They moved only a few steps at a time, as quietly as possible, looking for the pawed-earth scrapes in the leaves that held the mating signals for the does. Does were drawn to them because of the smell of buck urine in the scrapes and rubs on small saplings of the scent glands on the necks of the males. Once the hunters located one of these, they hid themselves to wait for a buck checking the scrape, or a doe drawn to them.

As the two crept along as quietly as they could, suddenly Caleb stopped and hissed, "There's a big buck scrape just over to my left near that big pin oak. See it?"

"Yes, I see it," Isiah said quietly. "I'll tell you what. I'll work my way to about twenty-five yards on the other side of the tree and you stay here. That way we can waylay the buck or doe as they approach the scrape. It should be easy to get a shot because their "juices" will be flowing so strong, they probably won't even see or sense us."

"That is a good idea. I swear, if I didn't know better, I'd say you probably did this before in England to the King's deer," whispered Caleb.

"You're very close to the truth, brother," whispered Isiah back.

Two hours they waited; nothing but a squirrel barking at them and birds scolding them.

Suddenly, a loud, shrill, bugling, sound rent the still morning air. Both of the hunters were startled to say the least. Heck! They were frightened!

The bugling sound rang out again, and it sounded closer, but a bit to their northern side. Both hunters strained their necks and entire bodies to try to catch a glimpse of the strange animal. The hunters moved slowly toward each other to try to get control of the situation. As they neared each other, Caleb hissed, "Did you ever hear such a sound?"

"You heard it, too?" retorted Isiah. "What in the world do you think it was?"

"I don't know, but I'm game to try to find out, if you are?" replied Caleb.

With Caleb leading the way, the hunters, stepping high so as not to rustle the leaves on the forest floor, moved in the direction of the last whistle. Suddenly, about twenty yards away, it looked to as if a small tree's limbs were moving through the undergrowth. The animal stepped into an open space in the woods and stopped, head up, sensing the air for a scent of the intruders that had disturbed him into bugling. Neither of the hunters could hardly breathe so rapidly was their adrenalin racing. The animal was a huge deer of some unknown species to them. It had huge antlers that extended straight up from its head for several inches, then flattened out for a space. Then, the huge forks extended out and above them for at least three feet in a palmate pattern. Not only were his antlers so huge, but his body was reddish-gray, except for its hind quarters which were a yellowish-white.

Suddenly, the huge deer let another shrill, bugle

sound. The hunters looked at each other. Almost inaudibly, Caleb said, "Shall we take him?"

"Yes," replied Isiah. "If the meat is edible, we certainly should, or we'll all starve."

Slowly, the two hunters raised their weapons simultaneously. Almost as one, the muskets fired. For an instant, the hunters were unable to see what had happened through the smoke from the firing of the guns. As the smoke cleared, they could see the huge beast lying still on the forest floor not moving a muscle.

"We had better reload before we go over there. He may not be dead and get up and attack us," cautioned Caleb.

As they approached the carcass, it became evident that the huge animal would never rise again. After several minutes admiring their kill, Isiah said, "You go and get the others. Tell them to get all of their gear together, and to come on up here to set up camp. That will be easier than carrying all of this meat back there."

The remainder of that night and the next day were spent in skinning the animal and cutting the huge carcass into transportable loads. They also enjoyed a full stomach for the first time in several days.

Now, the de facto leader, Luke Gibson, spoke up. "In this heat, the meat will be unfit to eat in only two or three days seeing that we don't have any way of preserving it, that is, no salt. What we need to do is to make a form of jerky out of as much of it as we can. It won't taste very palatable, but it will keep us alive until we find some other food source. We'll find an open area and spread out the sail on the ground. Then, we'll slice the meat into thin strips and dry it on the sail in the hot sun."

One of the hunters replied, "That's a good idea. We saw such an open space just down south of here, only about one hundred yards away. I'll take a couple of men with me and the sail and spread it out. We'll carry the slices to the sail as fast as it can be sliced off of the carcass."

After three days of feasting on the fresh meat and drying "jerky," it was apparent that it was time to move on west. How were they to be sure that it was indeed "west" that they were traveling? It was by the age-old method of navigating by the positions of the sun, the moon, and Polaris, the North Star. Of course, their experience as sailors made them experts at this method. But when the sky was overcast for two or three days at a time, this method became haphazard at best. This often caused them to drift off course a bit.

This, coupled with the difficulty of following the best route through the virgin forest, caused them to veer off of due west, hence to "wander," severely at times, for several days which slowed their progress west. Fortunately, in the first part of their trek, the path of their journey, for the most part, did not present them with any great difficulty. Due to the summer heat, all of the streams and creeks and "small" rivers they encountered were shallow and narrow enough that they could easily wade them, even though at some of them, they had to search a bit for a wide, shallow, rocky, place to ford.

Chapter 7

Indians

Then the inevitable happened. The leader of the troupe for that day was John Powell. As they made their way slowly through the relatively dense forest, he saw it; a still-smoldering campfire. Animals don't make fires, so it must mean that the natives, the Indians, were nearby. Everyone was very quiet as they gathered around the smoldering embers. Luke Gibson spoke very quietly. "This means we will have to travel as quietly and as quickly as possible until we are sure we have put them well behind us. Therefore, try not to shuffle your feet in the leaves and no talking, or at least, very low talking, for the next two or three days."

The next day as they trudged along following the leader, Muhammed the Moor, suddenly they broke in to one of the meadows that was becoming more frequent. There, they saw several rows of huge, extremely broad leafed, green, plants about high. "These have to be planted because wild don't grow in neat rows like these," remarked Tom Collins.

"Yes, and they stink, too. These are stinking weeds. I wander what they're used for?" someone remarked.

"They can't be used for food. They must be used for medicine or something," remarked another.

"Well, don't bother them so that the natives will not know we are in the area, and let's get out of the area as quickly as possible," Luke Gibson said quietly. "Furthermore, we'll have to start posting a guard every night until we are well out of this territory."

The supreme tribal council of the Tuscaroras was meeting in emergency session. Chief Great Eagle was speaking. "It is confirmed that the Tuscarora land has been violated by outside intruders like those never seen before. Their skin is as white as light-color flint stone except for two that are black. Silent Deer has seen them near the stinking weed field. We do not know if they mean us harm or not, at this time. As for weapons, Silent Deer could not see any bows and arrows or spears, but two of them were carrying long, brownish sticks, and they all had shiny objects at their waists. But we can take no chances. We do not know how strong their medicine is, or if they even have any. But we must take no chances. What do the members of the council have to say on this topic?"

Strong Bear, after several seconds had passed, rose slowly to his feet. "Chief Great Eagle is right. We can take no chances. We must act now. Let us have our best bowmen shoot some arrows into one of the white ones. If he is able to survive the arrows, then we know they have strong medicine, and we can meet again to discuss how we must deal with them." Strong Bear sat back down and crossed his ankles and sat as before, staring straight in front of him.

Red Fox slowly rose to a standing position. "I think Strong Bear is right. We must know if they have strong medicine before we take them prisoner." And he slowly sat down with great solemnity.

Chief Great Eagle now spoke again. "We must get our five best bowmen to do what has been agreed on. So let it be done."

The next morning, the travelers rose early and hurriedly got their gear together. Without eating anything, they got into single file with two of them, Caleb Goins and John Powell, the two best marksmen, bringing up the front and rear armed with the loaded muskets. The five warriors were already lying in ambush position. Hidden behind the largest oak trees they found strategically situated, the ambushers waited silently for the approaching invaders. As the last of them passed by the hidden warriors, they stepped into the open and unleashed their arrows almost simultaneously. All five arrows found their marks into the back of John Powell who took two more steps, then pitched forward to the ground never uttering a sound.

At the sound of the twangs of the bows and the whiz of the arrows in flight, all of the other nine whites whirled around just in time to see John Powell stumble forward to the leafy, forest, floor and fling the musket to one side. With cries of anguish and fear, they quickly surrounded John's prostrate body, oblivious to the danger lurking somewhere nearby. It was quite obvious that John would never rise again.

"Quickly, now. We must leave this area as fast as possible," said Luke Gibson.

"But what about John? Shouldn't we bury him?" asked Isiah Mullins.

"We don't have time. We are in great peril here. We must leave now," Luke answered. "Let's go. And Caleb, you bring up the rear. Isiah, you carry John's weapon and lead the way."

The five Indian bowmen hurriedly reported back to the great Tuscarora council. "They have no strong medicine, "reported White Bird. "The one we shot died without making a sound. We can take them as prisoners, and they can carry our water, skin our game, and cook for us."

"So let it be done," replied Chief Great Eagle. "But do not harm them, or they will be useless to us." The band of warriors who were dispatched to bring the whites to the village, had decided to simply surround the whites and make them prisoners, by surprise, if possible.

The Indians set up a ring of braves surrounding a small clearing the whites were sure to cross and waited patiently for them to get into the middle of it. As the line of whites neared the center of the small meadow, the Indians stepped out silently, no war whoops or anything, and advanced toward the whites. Needless-to-say, the whites were stunned, petrified, not knowing what to do. To fight the overwhelming number of warriors would be foolish, even suicidal, so they just waited silently as the Indians got closer and closer. Now, they were there.

White Bird, the leader of the band, stepped forward and grabbed the musket in the hands of Caleb Goins who refused to let go of it. During the ensuing struggle, Caleb still had his finger on the already cocked musket. Suddenly, the musket discharged making a thunderous boom and emitting a tremendous cloud of powder smoke. The round from the weapon struck the warrior standing beside of White Bird squarely in the chest killing him instantly. The terrified Indians turned and fled the scene in horror.

When the breathless braves ran back into their village, White Bird ran into the council hut and breathlessly shouted to Great Eagle and the other tribal leaders, "The whites do have great medicine! Running Deer was killed by one of the thunder sticks without it ever touching him. We must let the white eyes alone and hope they soon leave our hunting grounds!"

"So let it be done," replied Great Eagle. And so it was done.

Chapter 8

The Great River

"Are we never going to get to that great river De Soto wrote about? Just how far is it? We've been out here for several weeks now and no sign of a great, not even a small, great river?" These were typical of the increased grumbling among the men nowadays. Dissatisfaction was growing daily.

Much of the complaining was directed toward Luke Gibson, whom the others had permitted to become their nominal leader. "He's leading us to perdition, for sure," was a constant refrain.

Every night that was clear, Luke checked their latitude location as closely as possible. However, the most important calculation, their longitude, was impossible to ascertain. So, exactly how far west they had actually traveled was a mere guess. They were probably averaging about ten miles per day. On some days they averaged more, on some days less, and sometimes, not at all. The two best marksmen were keeping them in supply of venison and wild turkey. However, they would soon have to begin rationing their powder and shot due to the dwindling supply. What they needed badly was salt, but none was available. The farther and farther they went west, the less and less the pine forest prevailed, and gradually the landscape had turned to a hardwood, deciduous, forest. Unless it was raining, or threatening to rain, the men simply slept on the forest floor amid the soft leaves, eschewing the use of the sail tent. They subsisted on a diet of venison, wild turkey, wild apples, and wild berries of several different species. Only occasionally did they see any signs of Indians such as abandoned campfires and stripped, deer carcasses. Once they came upon a meadow that had tall, green stalks with long narrow blades. And on the stalks, about four feet from the ground, were two oblong, round objects enclosed in green husks. Once again, it was evident that they had been planted because they were also planted in rows like the large green, broad-leafed plants they had encountered several days before. Hence, they felt relatively safe. The days had assumed a certain routine.

Chapter 9

The Devil

The routine continued until one bright, starlit, night when they happened to camp in a small, circular, clearing in the woods. They all noticed that there was a well-trodden trail around the little clearing, but all assumed it was a frequent camping site for Indians in the area, and the trodden circle was created as a result of some kind of ritual that the Indians observed.

That night was routine as they all prepared for the night's rest. They spread out the sail because the ground was a bit damp from a brief shower earlier that afternoon. All of their backpacks were stored inside the circle. After a particularly rigorous day on the trail, they retired rather early. This was one of those days. Soon, they all were in a relatively deep, sound, sleep. But the next morning was a morning they would never forget.

Upon awakening, to a man, all of their belongings were scattered helter-skelter outside the circular, trodden, ring. Obviously, they had been thrown from the inside of the circle. Even the shoes of the men who had taken them off for sleep were thrown outside the circle. But the biggest mystery was that even the sail they had been sleeping on now lay in a heap there as well. The stunned, former sleepers just stood in dismay at the entire situation. Who or what could have done this, especially without their knowing it? An Indian perhaps, or one of their own number for a joke? As they inquired of each other, someone commented, "Well, it's the devil of a mystery." "That's it," chimed in another. "It was the devil, Old Scratch himself. This path around must be the devil's tramping ground! Let's gather up our belongings and get as far away from this place as possible!"

Chapter 10

Death of a Compatriot

The group of men now continued to move steadily west. The land, once flat, was beginning to be a bit uneven with low hills now predominating. Once, after standing on the top of one of these low hills, they espied a rather large meadow at its base. After resting up a bit from their climb up, they made their way down to the bottom. As they began to cross the open place, they began to notice large, wallowed-out spots in the natural grass and dirt, much like a horse would leave after a long day in a harness. Then there were the relatively large hoof prints about the size of two large deer hoof prints or a mature cow back in their old homelands. But it most likely was not cows because cows were not supposed to inhabit this part of the world. Even De Soto had not made mention of any wild cattle in his journals.

Just as they entered the woods on the side of the clearing, there it was, the animal. The dark brown, strange, beast was at least five feet tall and had a huge hump on its shoulders which created a slight sloping back to a smaller rump and a short tail. It had a large, shaggy, black-maned, neck and two rather short, curved black horns curving out from near its small ears. It also had parted hoofs, as the tracks in the meadow had indicated. As the travelers stood transfixed, they saw movement in the trees just beyond the animal they were admiring. Several others of the same species of animal were milling around in the underbrush. Suddenly, the gigantic bull winded the men. Raising his magnificent head, he sniffed the air, then let out several cacophonous snorts, lowered his head, and began to paw the ground. Then he charged! The men scattered in all directions. But the young former cabin boy, Tom, was the unlucky one whom the beast concentrated on. He ran the boy down from behind, gored him viciously with first one horn, then the other. Neither of the instruments of death struck a vital spot or organ, but his buttocks, hips and thighs were badly mauled. As the fleeing others saw what was happening, they all turned to go help Tom, but were stopped in their tracks by a shout from one of the musket marksman, Isiah Mullins. Leveling his long weapon, he quickly took careful aim and shot the huge animal just behind its left shoulder. Although struck in the heart, the huge animal ran about twenty-five yards before toppling over.

Now, all of the men turned their attention to the wounded cabin boy. Tom was lying face down on the ground still alive, but bleeding badly from his horrific wounds. They all realized that unless they could get the bleeding stopped, the young boy would die. And without regaining consciousness, that is just what happened about thirty minutes later. After Luke said a few appropriate words over his lifeless body, they gently buried him in a shallow grave, which they had laboriously dug with their belt knives, far from his London home.

Chapter 11

The First Mountain

Now, it seemed that the hills were becoming low mountains. From one vantage point the men could see two or three low mountains, not hills, definitely mountains, but there were none others around as far as they could see. These were very old mountains, highly eroded over the epochs of time. In fact, these would turn out to be the oldest range of mountains in North America. Having climbed to the top of the highest mountain for a better view west, the travelers were disappointed to see nothing but the continuation of low, rolling hills west as far as the human eye can see. What they had hoped to see, of course, was the great river, but that was a long time off.

Chapter 12

Old Lucifer

As they descended the tallest mountain, they sat down to rest and make camp for the night. As they relaxed sitting on the leaves, suddenly to the left of them near an old fallen tree, came a peculiar, dry, shell-like, rattle. All eyes turned toward the sound. The leaves moved slightly very near the ancient bole. Out of pure curiosity, they all rose slowly to their feet starring toward the rattling sound and moving leaves. Now, they were within five feet of the racket. Isiah Mullins picked up a long branch and slowly raked away the leaves revealing a huge, blackish, diamond-striped, snake.

All eyes were transfixed on the monstrous serpent. As Isiah raked at the leaves once again, the serpent struck viciously, sinking his teeth deep into the stick. "I wonder if he is poisonous," said Isiah.

"Well, I don't care to be the one to find out on," said Muhammed, one of the Moors, in broken English.

"I don't want to sleep here tonight. Let's move on to some distance away," spoke up Caleb Goins.

"I, for one, am just glad that these things aren't native to England," spoke up Luke Gibson.

Chapter 13

The First River

"I wonder if this is the great river De Soto was describing in his annals." Pierre Le Bon spoke first as they assembled on the banks of the muddy river.

"I don't think it could be. According to De Soto, a man could hardly see the other side of the great river. This river is only about sixty or seventy yards wide all along its course," responded Caleb. "De Soto has seen many rivers, and I doubt he would describe this as a great river."

"I agree with you," replied Luke. "This is not De Soto's great river. We will just have to cross it in some manner, that's all. Besides, it seems to be flowing southeast anyway."

And so the die was cast; but how to cross it and not get someone drowned?

"We can't swim it with our backpacks on for two reasons. First, it would be impossible to keep our packs dry, and second, the packs might get so soggy and heavy the current may sweep us away," mused Isiah Mullins.

"The only other course I see is a raft. Luckily, we have the two axes. We won't need more than three small logs bound together. We can swim along-side holding on to and steering the raft which will have all of our gear on it safe out of the water," replied Luke Gibson. "Poplar trees are the lightest, so let's cut three poplars and bind them together with some of the large vines that are just back there. I saw them as we arrived," continued Luke.

Soon, the axes were ringing and the poplars were falling. Each one was measured, cut off at the right length, carried to the edge of the river, and deposited on the bank. There, with much difficulty, they were secured together rather clumsily with the hard-to-manage vines. But, at last, it was done.

Now, the de facto leader, Luke Gibson, spoke up again. "Obviously, we cannot attempt a crossing with the river so high and muddy. We'll have to wait until the water clears and drops several feet before a crossing is attempted. So, let's camp here for the night, and perhaps the men with the fish hooks can catch us a mess of fish for breakfast."

The men spent a fitful night. No one got much sleep because of the swarms of mosquitos that buzzed along the river banks. Most of them slept as close to the fire as possible, hoping that the smoke would give some relief from the mosquitos. But nothing seemed to work for long.

Most of the men were up early because nothing had seemed to work against the mosquitos. They all ambled over to the river bank, and all drew the same conclusion. The river was still running high and muddy, but not nearly as high as the night before. It would take a few more hours for the crossing conditions to become right. Meanwhile for breakfast they feasted on a meal of white fish and catfish.

By noon, the water level in the river had dropped to its normal level, and the current was practically nonexistent. It was time to cross. Each one attached his pack securely to the top side of the three logs that made up the raft. Then, they gingerly slid the contraption into the water and with four men on each side, they began the crossing. Some of the way, the water was so shallow that the men could walk, but at other times they had to swim. Soon, they were docking the raft in the mud on the other bank and gathering their gear from it. All was well.

Chapter 14

Another River and Another Mountain

They headed due west once more. But soon, once again, they stood on the bank of another river just as wide and forbidding, but not as muddy as the one they had forded only a few days ago. It was "Plan A" again. A poplar raft, guiding it and swimming to the other side, but this time they did not have to wait because the river was running at its normal level. Once again, it was a big breakfast of fish and heading west again, leaving the country of the river-dwelling Indians.

For three days the travelers moved slightly northwest. Here the hills were becoming steeper and steeper. Then, one afternoon, Abbad the Moor was the first to see it. It was a huge mountain by far the biggest and highest most of them had ever seen, even in all of their travels. It reminded some of them of a huge elephant's back and head, especially the head. To others, it looked like a volcano with a huge stopper jammed in the crater.

As the party drew nearer to the mountain, they could see a faint trail of blue smoke curling upward from the crest of the huge, granite stopper. This could mean only one thing; Indians who were probably performing a religious ritual or communicating with some of their own tribe. Also, in the distance they could see the tops of a range of low, hazy-blue, mountains, and their hearts sank. They were practically starved and poorly clad and carrying heavy packs. How would they ever get over these mountains?

For several days, the eight men struggled up and down the mountains trying to cross in as many low gaps as possible to make the going easier. The physical exertion was rapidly drawing the last vestiges of energy from their emaciated bodies. For the last several nights the temperature had been dropping significantly, so much so that they had to have a fire all night. This was a portent of their greatest obstacle yet, winter. They simply could not survive a winter in the open. They would surely freeze and starve to death. Then, the miracle, though in disguise, happened.

One day as they were crossing a large creek, a huge Indian stepped out of the foliage on the far bank. For a full minute the whites and the Indian starred at each other. Now, several more Indians joined the oversized one on the creek bank. The big brave extended his hand toward Mohammed who was standing on a rock in mid-stream. For a long moment, Muhammed hesitated. Then, he slowly extended his own black hand toward the brown hand. The huge

Indian grasped Muhammed's hand in a firm grip and lifted and pulled him on across the creek to the bank. Turning back to the other white men, he helped each one to the other side of the stream in the same manner. Next, he motioned with his hand that the whites were to follow him. As the Indians began to walk away, the whites just stood there hesitating to follow. Several of the Indians then turned and motioned them to come on. The whites began to follow, fearing that they had no alternative.

Chapter 15

In Custody

The whites could count, and the numbers definitely were not in their favor. They were vastly outnumbered, so they quietly fell into single file behind the Indians. Each one was left to his own thoughts. How is this going to turn out? Will we all be horribly murdered? However, most of them despaired of ever surviving the ordeal they had been experiencing anyway. Most had resigned themselves to dying in the trackless forest by now. Some were not as morose as the others, however. They were taking notice that the Indians were not acting warlike. They weren't carrying weapons, and there had been no aggressive behavior and no war whoops. Also, there was not any markings on them that might have been war paint.

After trudging along the mountain paths for most of the rest of the day, the mountains began to become lower and more spread out. They had crossed the highest mountains. As the sun began to set, they began to smell smoke. Soon, they approached a large meadow in which were several rectangular, thatched huts with roofs made of reed mats and large, thin sheets of birch bark. Some huts were large and some small. In the center of them was a large campfire. Smoke was rising from numerous small cooking fires near the entrances of most of them. As the column entered the village, the inhabitants stopped what they were doing and stared at the strangely colored people, black and white together.

The leader of the Indians stopped at the entrance of the largest thatched hut and motioned for the others to wait for him as he went inside. There, he found the entire tribal council presided over by the chief, Black Crow, sitting on mats of reeds, and passing a stinking weed smoking pipe between them. The leader of the Indian band who had accosted the whites, Big Beaver, approached the council and spoke in a mundane voice trying to hide his excitement. "Great Chief Black Crow, we have the strange ones we have been observing for several days outside."

"This is good," replied Chief Black Crow. "We will go and see these strange-looking men the gods have sent among us," he said, laying aside the smoking pipe, and rising laboriously from his cross-legged, sitting, position. "Who knows, they may be gods themselves, so we must treat them well."

Chief Black Crow walked down the line of whites and blacks, looking each one up and down. As he came to Isiah Mullins, he stopped and reached and touched his forearm and rubbed it vigorously. Then, he turned to the other braves and grunted something.

When he came to the black Moor, Abbad, he did the same thing. Apparently satisfied, the chief turned to the other Indians and spoke rapidly. What was going to happen next, wondered all of the "captives." Big Beaver motioned for them all to follow him once again. He led them to another rather large, rectangular, thatched, dwelling and indicated that they were to enter. Bending low, each one stepped through the opening on to the woven, reed mats provided. Suddenly, through the entrance walked several Indian women carrying wooden bowls filled with corn pone, cooked venison, melons, and vegetables and set them before the astonished, former, travelers. As the whites just sat and stared, Big Beaver motioned for them to eat.

There was no way for the Indians and the whites to communicate except by the simplest physical motions such as hand movements and facial expressions. As darkness approached, Big Beaver indicated that they were to sleep there for the night.

Chapter 16

The Showdown

Early the next morning, Big Beaver, standing in the opening of the hut where the men had slept, motioned the men to follow him once more. This is it, most of them thought, as they rose stiffly to their feet. They followed Big Beaver to the center of the compound where a constant fire was kept burning. Standing by the fire, were all members of the tribal council including Chief Black Crow. Laying on the ground before them were the two axes, the two muskets, and the Dutch oven and skillet. Chief Black Crow picked up one of the axes and handed it to Luke Gibson and grunted and gestured as to what it was. Luke turned to the wood pile and picked out a sizeable branch. Then, in one mighty flash of the axe, he cut the branch in to two pieces. Grunts of approval were emitted by all of the Indians. Next, Chief Black Crow handed one of the muskets to Luke. Luke turned and carried a piece of the firewood to about thirty paces away. Returning to his original spot, he raised the musket and fired, knocking the targeted piece of fire wood hither and yon. At the explosion, most of the Indians let out a whoop and staggered backward in amazement. Next, the chief handed the Dutch oven to Luke. Luke removed the lid and took a piece of jerky from his pocket, placed it inside the oven, and replaced the lid. Now, he placed the entire apparatus into the middle of the fire. Picking up the skillet, he repeated the process. This elicited loud grunts of approval from all the Indians.

Chief Black Crow addressed his fellow tribesmen gathered around. "These men have strong medicine. They are messengers from the gods. The gods have sent them to us to reward our obedience to them. Treat the messengers well."

Chapter 17

To Go or to Stay

A mysterious enigma now began for both the Indians and the whites. What should happen next? For the next several days, the whites wandered about the village learning how the Indians lived their daily lives. They were treated with great deference and respect by all of the Indians. Then, one morning they woke up to find a heavy snow had fallen during the night. Quickly, Luke called a meeting of all of his compatriots. "We sure can't travel any more this winter. If the Indians will let us, we'll stay here until next spring. Then, we can travel west again and find the great river," he said in urgent tones. "Besides, we must have clothes that will keep us warm against the winter cold, and we have none. The Indians are well prepared for the cold with their clothes of animal pelts and moccasins and leggings of deer hide. We have to convince the natives that we need clothes. And we can't do this by being aggressive or unhospitable. We must curry their favor. They already hold us as special from their gods because of our white and black skins and our weapons and tools. We must show them how to use our tools, how to chop wood with the axes, cook in the Dutch oven and skillet, and hunt with the muskets, at least, until we run out of ammunition.

That's what they all agreed to do, and an unusual rapport was established with the Indians. The Indians provided them with clothes made from animal pelts, food, and a large, thatched hut.

However, human nature being what it is, by spring, five of the eight men had "married" Indian maids. Although they still talked occasionally of the great river, no one seemed very interested in returning to the endless, trackless, forest where they most likely would perish. To go back east was certain death. Their former lives were over. Their only recourse now was to begin new ones. The great river had never been just over the horizon. They had taken the gamble of going west, and they had lost. Soon, the great river was forgotten as they reared their families and created a new society in the wilderness, the Melungeon society.

And, as they say, the rest is history.

The Trek Westward

Land of the Melungeons

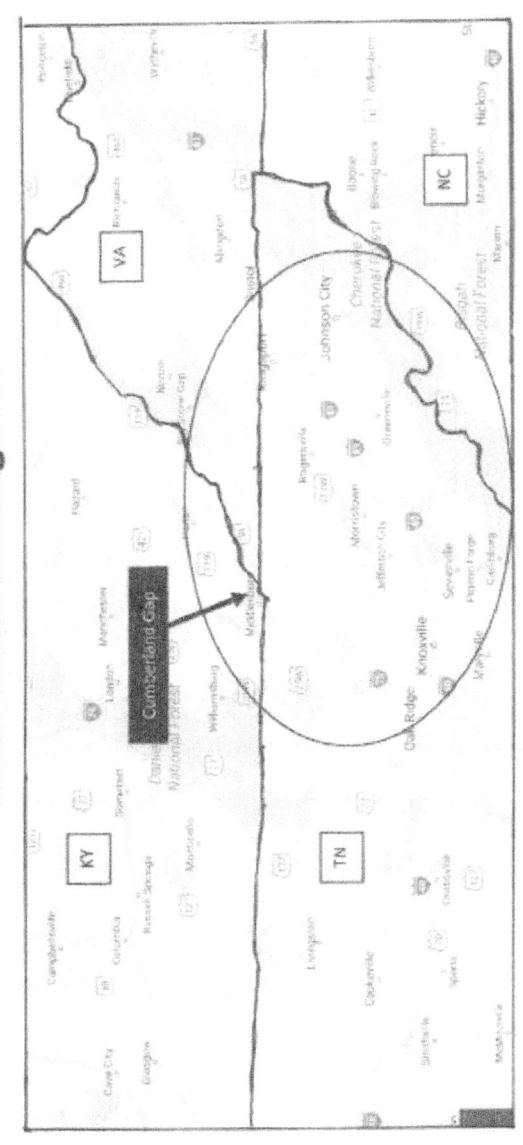

Melungeons

A TYPICAL MALUNGEON.
(Drawn from a photograph taken for Will Allen Dromgoole.)

Will Allen Dromgoole's drawing of a Melungeon at Newman's Ridge, Tennessee, c. 1890

Gary Powers

Gary Powers

Native American Village

Epilogue

It is rather obvious to historians that the tired, hungry, emaciated, early travelers, where ever they were from, were befriended by a tribe of sympathetic Native Americans who took them into their society at least as equals. They would surely have perished, if this had not been the case. They found a good, safe, life there, and "married" Indian women and reared families. They were extremely fortunate that the Indians in question were peaceful and not war-like, as were the plains Indians, such as the Pawnees and the Comanches. The offspring from these unions married each other and other Indian women. Down through the years, this practice created the peculiar, multi-racial, but mostly white people, who came to be called the Melungeons.

Today, it is becoming chic to be identified as a Melungeon. This was not the case in most of the unique history of these people. In the past, they have been thought of and treated as second class citizens. Some etymologists believe that the English word "melengin" from which the modern word Melungeon is derived meant "guile," "deceit," or "ill intent." Sometimes, the word meant "harbored evil people." Today, there is a renewed interest in these mysterious people.

Postscript

The two large animals, the elk and the buffalo, usually referred to as the woodland buffalo, described in the narrative really did inhabit the eastern forests in the 1500s, but obviously not in the same numbers as on the Great Plains. Since then, they have been hunted to extinction.

Credits

"Dances with Wolves", Motion Picture, Directed by Kevin Costner, 1990

The World of the American Indian, National Geographic Society, Washington DC, 1979

Publicly Available information on the Internet

I would like to thank the staff of the public library of High Point, North Carolina for their help in my research for this book. They located all of the pertinent information that I used, and made a packet of copies of it for me. It should be noted that I did not use any other books for my research.

Other Books by Dr. Larry G. Morgan

Ivy

Mountain Born, Mountain Molded

Appalachian Mountain Memories

Golf Poems for Everyone

Old Time Religion in the Southern Appalachians

Strange Life-Struggling with the Mysteries of OCD

Joseph's Son

The Journey

A Time line for Creation and Other Essays

Made in the USA
Coppell, TX
14 February 2022

73588291R00059